KT-558-048

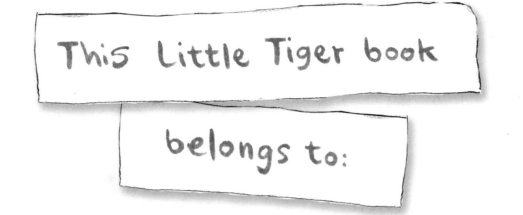

This Little Tiger book

belongs to:

_____

_____

_____

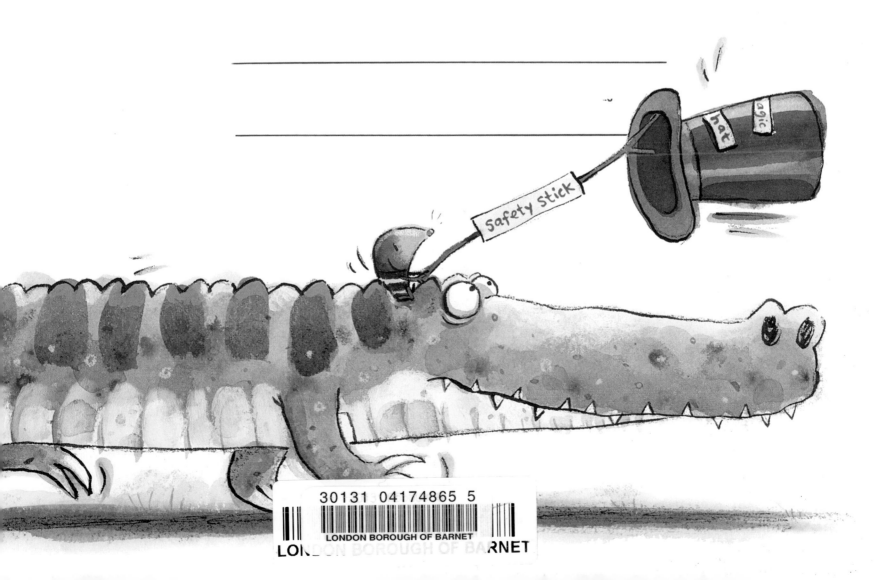

safety stick

30131 04174865 5

LONDON BOROUGH OF BARNET
LONDON BOROUGH OF BARNET

For Levi
Because you're never too old for bunnies.

LITTLE TIGER PRESS
1 The Coda Centre,
189 Munster Road, London SW6 6AW
www.littletiger.co.uk

First published in Great Britain 2016
This edition published 2016
Text and illustrations copyright © Tim Warnes 2016
Visit Tim Warnes at www.ChapmanandWarnes.com
Tim Warnes has asserted his right
to be identified as the author and illustrator of this work
under the Copyright, Designs and Patents Act, 1988
A CIP catalogue record for this book is available from the British Library
All rights reserved

ISBN 978-1-84869-202-2
LTP/1400/1344/1015
Printed in China
2 4 6 8 10 9 7 5 3 1

"Missing Hat"

Do not touch!
If found, contact
THE GREAT RENATO
IMMEDIATELY

reed

damselfly

friend

WARNING!
THIS BOOK MAY CONTAIN RABBITS!

tim warnes

LITTLE TIGER PRESS
London

coracle

lily

lily pad

Mole loved labelling things.

All sorts of things.

Anything really.

It was his absolute top thing to do.

His best friend, the Lumpy-Bumpy Thing,
was rather good at it too.

Woodpecker

nest

oak

mossy

leaf

spider

web

green

rhubarb

vegetable

patch

carrots

No entry

lettuce

log

lettuce

Slimy

bark

rough

Sna

One day, the two friends spotted something unusual on the path.

"**Look!**" gasped Mole. "A **snow bunny!** I've seen **brown** bunnies and **black** bunnies and **grey** bunnies before, but I've never seen a white one."

It was very mysterious indeed.

pinecone

butterfly

fungus

rock

Mole started to label the bunny. But it bounced away.

"Stop that bunny!" cried Mole.

So the Lumpy-Bumpy Thing chased after it.

The Lumpy-Bumpy Thing came back
wearing an interesting-looking hat.
The hat already had a label:
WARNING! Do not touch!

"Quick! Take it off!"
cried Mole. "It could be dangerous."

But the Lumpy-Bumpy Thing
just giggled. Then it lifted up
the hat.

WARNING!
Do not
touch!

flopsy

cute

There, on its head, was another
bunny, with a very tickly tail.

"Holey moley!" gasped Mole.
"That hat's magic!"

The bunny jumped down
and gave Mole
a great, big snuggle.
"I suppose it's
safe enough," Mole
grinned. "After all,
they ARE just bunnies."

On-off, on-off went the magic hat.
"Look how many bunnies you've made!"
exclaimed Mole. "I'm going to number them so we
can play Bunny Bingo!"

The Lumpy-Bumpy Thing was in Bunny Heaven!

But Mole was not. Those **naughty** bunnies kept swapping places and muddling themselves up.

It was all **very confusing.**

"Ten, seven, nine, five – **wait!** That's **not right**,"
grumbled Mole. **"Keep still!"**

But the bunnies wouldn't listen.

Bunny after bunny
jumped out from the hat.

"97, 98, 99, 100!"

What had started out
as a Bit Of Fun quickly
became a Bit
Of A Problem.

"Make it STOP!" hollered Mole.

The Lumpy-Bumpy
Thing tried pushing
the bunnies back
in the hat. But they
were too wriggly.

It tried scaring
them away.
But they weren't
bothered at all.

"Look at this mess!" wailed Mole.
The bunnies had eaten all the flowers
They'd dug hundreds of holes.
And now they were pooping all
over the place!

"Stop it!
Bad bunnies!"
cried mole.

Then the Lumpy-Bumpy Thing spotted Something Terrible! Number 54 was heading straight for Mole's vegetable patch . . .

Mole ran after him.
"Give me that carrot!"
he demanded.

They **tugged** and they **pulled,**

and they **pulled** and they **tugged,** until . . .

DOING!

Number 54 let go.

"Ha ha! Got it!" shouted Mole, waving the carrot triumphantly in the air. The other bunnies stopped and stared and twitched their noses . . .

. . . then they **CHARGED!**

"RUN FOR IT!"
yelled Mole.

But the Lumpy-Bumpy Thing stumbled.
Mole's carrot sailed through the air . . .

. . . and fell with a **plop!**
into the magic hat.
One of the bunnies
dived in after it . . .
and disappeared!

"Hooray!" cried Mole. "Quick! Grab some
more carrots!"
So the two friends started hurling
them into the hat. And one by one,
the bunnies followed.

"Ten, nine, eight, seven, six, five, four, three, two, one, ZERO BUNNIES!" declared Mole. "We did it!"

The Lumpy-Bumpy Thing
peered nervously
into the hat.

"Don't worry," said Mole.
"They've gone now."

Very carefully they
carried it back to
where they'd found it.

"We don't want any
more trouble, do we?"
said Mole.

But the Lumpy-Bumpy Thing
was looking at something
unusual in the grass –
something with a label on it.
   "Don't touch that!"
gulped Mole.

But it was too late . . .

"Holey moley!" cried Mole.
"Not again!"

WARNING!
THESE BOOKS MAY CONTAIN BRILLIANT STORIES!

special

I Love You as BIG as the World

David Van Buren   Tim Warnes

exciting

Hands off MY HONEY!

Jane Chapman
Tim Warnes

The Great Cheese Robbery

Tim Warnes

mischievous

DANGEROUS!

tim warnes

bumpy
sharp
stripy
rough
spiky

With over 100 free stickers!

funny

For information regarding any of the above titles or for our catalogue, please contact us:
Little Tiger Press, 1 The Coda Centre, 189 Munster Road, London SW6 6AW
Tel: 020 7385 6333 • E-mail: contact@littletiger.co.uk • www.littletiger.co.uk